Franklin Celebrates

From an episode of the animated TV series *Franklin* produced by Nelvana Limited, Neurones France s.a.r.l. and Neurones Luxembourg S.A.

Based on the Franklin books by Paulette Bourgeois and Brenda Clark.

TV tie-in adaptation written by Sharon Jennings and illustrated by Sean Jeffrey, Sasha McIntyre and Alice Sinkner.

Based on the TV episode *Franklin Migrates*, written by Karen Moonah.

Franklin

Kids Can Press acknowledges the financial support of the Government of Ontario, through the Ontario Media Development Corporation's Ontario Book Initiative; the Ontario Arts Council; the Canada Council for the Arts; and the Government of Canada, through the BPIDP, for our publishing activity.

Published in Canada by
Kids Can Press Ltd.
29 Birch Avenue
Toronto, ON M4V 1E2

Published in the U.S. by
Kids Can Press Ltd.
2250 Military Road
Tonawanda, NY 14150

www.kidscanpress.com

Series editor: Tara Walker
Edited by Jennifer Stokes

Printed and bound in China

This book is smyth sewn casebound.

CM 05 0 9 8 7 6 5 4 3 2 1
CM PA 05 0 9 8 7 6 5 4 3 2 1

Library and Archives Canada Cataloguing in Publication Data

Jennings, Sharon
    Franklin celebrates / Sharon Jennings ; illustrated by Sean Jeffrey, Sasha McIntyre, Alice Sinkner.

(A Franklin TV storybook)
The character Franklin was created by Paulette Bourgeois and Brenda Clark.
ISBN 1-55337-501-7 (bound).

I. Jeffrey, Sean II. McIntyre, Sasha III. Sinkner, Alice IV. Bourgeois, Paulette V. Clark, Brenda VI. Title. VII. Series: Franklin TV storybook.

PS8569.E563F7176 2005   jC813'.54   C2004-906025-2

Kids Can Press is a  Entertainment company

Franklin Celebrates

Kids Can Press

FRANKLIN could count by twos and tie his shoes. He knew the days of the week, the months of the year and the holidays in every season. Soon it would be Halloween. And just as Franklin was beginning to think about ghosts, goblins and jack-o'-lanterns, he was invited to a party for a holiday that he knew nothing about.

Franklin hurried home from school. A letter was waiting for him on the table.

Franklin tore open the envelope.

It was an invitation. Goose was having a Migration Eve party on the weekend.

"A party!" exclaimed Franklin.

He ran to find his parents.

Franklin showed his mother the invitation.

"What's Migration Eve?" he asked.

"It's a goose holiday," she replied. "It marks the day geese leave their summer homes and fly south for the winter."

Franklin was puzzled.

"But Goose doesn't migrate," he pointed out.

"Her family doesn't," agreed Franklin's mother. "But lots of her friends and relatives do."

"Maybe you can ask Goose about Migration Eve at school tomorrow," suggested Franklin's father.

But Goose wasn't at school the next day.

"This is a very special time for Goose," explained Mr. Owl. "She's helping her family get ready for the festivities."

Franklin told Mr. Owl that he was invited to the Migration Eve party.

"It's a wonderful celebration," said Mr. Owl. "Lots of geese will be there, old and young. There will be special food and songs and ... why, you'll probably be taught the migration dance!"

Franklin looked worried.

"There's a dance?" he asked.

After school, Franklin told his mother all about Migration Eve.

"There'll be lots of food I've never eaten," he grumbled. "And I'll have to sing songs I don't know, and then I'll have to learn a dance, and I don't want to dance."

Franklin took a big bite of his fly and jelly sandwich.

"And what if I have to talk to geese I don't know?" he added.

His mother smiled and gave him a hug.

"Don't worry, Franklin," she said. "Goose will make sure you have a good time."

The night before the party, Franklin said
his tummy was jumpy.

"Maybe I shouldn't go tomorrow," he said.
"I don't think I should eat strange food and
dance around."

"Oh, dear," said his mother, as she tucked
him into bed. "I was counting on your help
tomorrow. I want to make a blueberry pie
to send to Mrs. Goose."

Franklin sighed.

At least there'd be one thing at the party
he could eat.

In the morning, Franklin helped his mother
make two blueberry pies. Then he scrubbed
his face and hands and put on his best clothes.

"Now, remember to say please and thank
you," said his mother.

"And have fun," said his father.

Franklin nodded.

"But I'm not going to dance," he mumbled.

When Franklin arrived, Goose's home was overflowing with guests. Tables were set up on the lawn and piled high with food. A band played music, and goslings ran about everywhere, sneaking treats from the dessert table and scampering off to hide.

"Franklin!" cried Goose. "I'm so glad you're here."

Mrs. Goose took Franklin's pies.

"Thank you, Franklin," she said. "How thoughtful!"

Goose led Franklin across the lawn.

"First, let's eat," she said. "You have to try some of everything."

Franklin felt his tummy begin to flip-flop. But then he looked at the food.

"This food is all normal," he said.

Goose looked puzzled.

"Of course it's normal," she replied. "And it's yummy!"

Goose heaped Franklin's plate with a bit of everything.

"We always begin with ice cream," she explained. "That reminds us that the cold is coming. Then we have mashed potatoes. They're like the clouds we fly through on our way south. Then a cob of corn covered in butter – that's yellow for the sun on our wings."

Franklin ate and ate and listened to Goose talk about her traditions.

"And we finish with a donut. But you have to share it with someone. That means we're sharing our journey together."

Franklin smiled and gave half of his donut to Goose.

When Goose left to help her mother, she introduced Franklin to her grampy and gammy. Franklin sat down and wondered what to say.

"Is it hard to migrate?" he finally asked.

"Oh, very hard," replied Grampy. "And dangerous, too."

Then Grampy told one tale after another. Franklin listened wide-eyed to the scary stories. He laughed when Grampy told the funny story about how Great-Uncle Goosebert lost his tail feathers.

Grampy talked until he fell asleep.

"Thank you, Franklin," said Gammy. "You've been a wonderful listener, and Grampy loves to tell his tales."

Franklin grinned.

Soon, Goose came rushing over for Franklin.

"We're starting the migration dance. Come on!"

All the geese were in a V-formation on the lawn. Franklin tried to hang back, but Goose tugged on his arm. Soon, he was standing in formation with everyone else.

Stomp, stomp, stomp.
Clap, clap, clap.
Lift your wings
and flap, flap, flap.
Turn to the moon
and do-si-do.
Bow to where
the warm wind blows!
Shimmy, shimmy, shimmy.
Shake, shake, shake.
Now it's time to
Mi-i-grate!

In no time at all, Franklin was singing and stomping and laughing with the others.

When it was time for the real migration to begin, there were hugs and tears and shouted goodbyes. Those who were leaving lined up on the hillside.

Franklin stood beside Goose. They watched as the V-formation of geese flew across the moon.

"One day I will be with them, Franklin," whispered Goose.

Franklin smiled at his friend.

"I sure hope you invite me to your party," said
Franklin. "I wouldn't miss Migration Eve for anything!"